OUTSIDE AND INSIDE

RATS AND MICE

BY SANDRA MARKLE

ATHENEUM BOOKS FOR YOUNG READERS

NEW YORK   LONDON   TORONTO   SYDNEY   SINGAPORE

There are about three hundred different kinds of rats in the world. Some live in dry deserts. Others live where winters are long and snowy. Still others live in cities, like these brown rats. Some of them make their home alongside people in buildings, parks, and subways.

Look at the white-footed mouse, on the left, and the cotton rat on the right. The rat is much bigger. The main difference between mice and rats is size. Rats may be as much as fifteen times bigger than mice. Whatever their size, mice and rats have many things in common—one is big front teeth.

Check out the front teeth on this mole rat! Just like you, a rat's teeth have a hard coating of *enamel*. A rat's front teeth are much harder than yours, though—hard enough to *gnaw* through *bone* or wire. Unlike your teeth, a rat's front teeth also keep on growing longer. So as much as it gnaws, there is always new tooth material to replace what wears away.

See how the rat's mouth is closed behind its front teeth. Unlike you, a rat has a space between its front teeth and its big back teeth, or molars. By sucking its cheeks into this space, the rat seals out nutshells, wood chips, and dirt while it gnaws.

Look closely at the deer mouse's front feet. The long toes act like fingers, letting the mouse pick up and hold food. Rats and mice, though, lack a thumb. Try picking up something without using your thumb to see how hard it is.

A rat's back legs and feet help it get around. Its legs are bent while it is resting. So to jump, it straightens its legs. Some kinds of rats and mice, like this white-footed mouse, can jump straight up about seven times their body length. Imagine how high you could jump if you could jump that high.

Next, check out the rat's big back foot. You will see that each toe ends in a sturdy nail. The nails help the rat climb. Some rats that live where the weather is warm year-round make their *nests* in trees.

This rat is grooming its fur after swimming across a stream. Its big back feet helped the rat swim. By grooming, the rat spreads its natural body oil over its fur. This lets the hair shed water, keeping the rat's skin dry and warm.

Can you guess why this mother rat is holding up her long tail as she carries her baby?

Did you guess the rat's tail keeps her balanced? As the rat walks, she swings her tail from side to side.

Take a close look at the rat's tail. Rats can't sweat the way you can to cool off. So as a rat heats up, *blood* flow near the surface of its tail increases. Heat escapes from the blood through the skin, cooling off the rat.

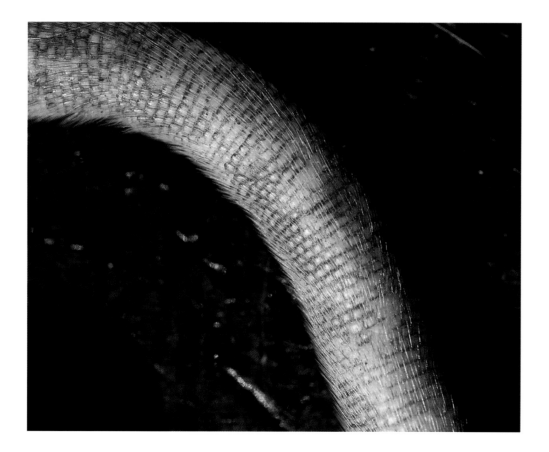

This X ray lets you peek inside a rat to see its bones. Just as a building has a strong framework to support it and give it shape, a rat's body, like yours, has a framework, too—a bony *skeleton.* See how many little bones there are? Like you, a rat can only bend where two bones meet. Having lots of bones lets it bend and move easily.

Wrap your fingers around your upper arm. Then bend and straighten it. The bulge you feel is *muscle.* Muscles attach to bones to move them. But muscles can only pull on bones, not push them. So to move, a rat's body, like yours, has pairs of muscles—one to pull out, one to pull back.

This rat is inside a house wall. Although it can see clearly for only about 15 centimeters (6 inches) around it, a rat can see better in the dark than you can. And with its eyes on the sides of its head, the rat can see nearly all the way around itself without turning its head. A rat can also feel where it's going. Like stretching out your arms as you walk through the dark, a rat fans out the whiskers around its nose to sense when a passage is getting narrow, possibly too narrow to squeeze through safely.

Look at the mouse listening for any sound that could mean danger. Its big ears can turn this way and that to catch sounds. Think what it would be like if your ears could do that!

Now, imagine the highest-pitched sound you've ever heard. Mice and rats can hear much higher-pitched sounds than that—sounds too high for your ears to detect.

Rats and mice eats lots of different kinds of food, such as corn, berries, seeds, birds' eggs, insects, and earthworms. A garbage pile is a feast for a rat. Some rats dine in groups but even then it's each rat for itself.

Mice and rats search for the safest way to travel. They mark their trails with their *urine* so they can quickly find their way even in the dark.

Of course, rats and mice always have to be ready to run and hide. Lots of animals—such as owls, hawks, weasels, and coyotes—count on eating them.

Like you, a rat gets the energy it needs to run and be active from its food. Look in the mirror and open your mouth. *Digestion,* or the breaking down of food, begins here. First, rats chew, grinding the food between their molars. Then a special liquid called *saliva* floods the food, starting to break it down.

Next, the mashed wad is swallowed. Then more digestive juices go to work, breaking down the food in the *stomach* and the *small intestine.* Finally, the food is broken down into chemical building blocks, or *nutrients,* ready for use. These nutrients pass into the bloodstream and are carried to all parts of the rat's body.

What's left over moves into the *large intestine.* There most of the water passes into the bloodstream. Some rats and mice get much of the water they need to live from the food they eat. What's left is passed out as waste pellets.

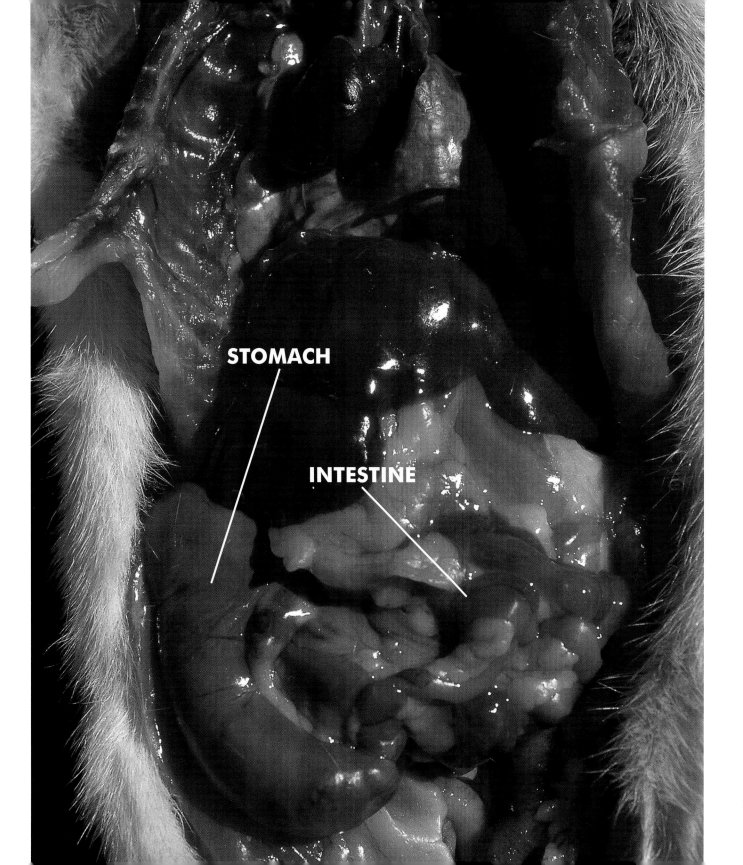

STOMACH

INTESTINE

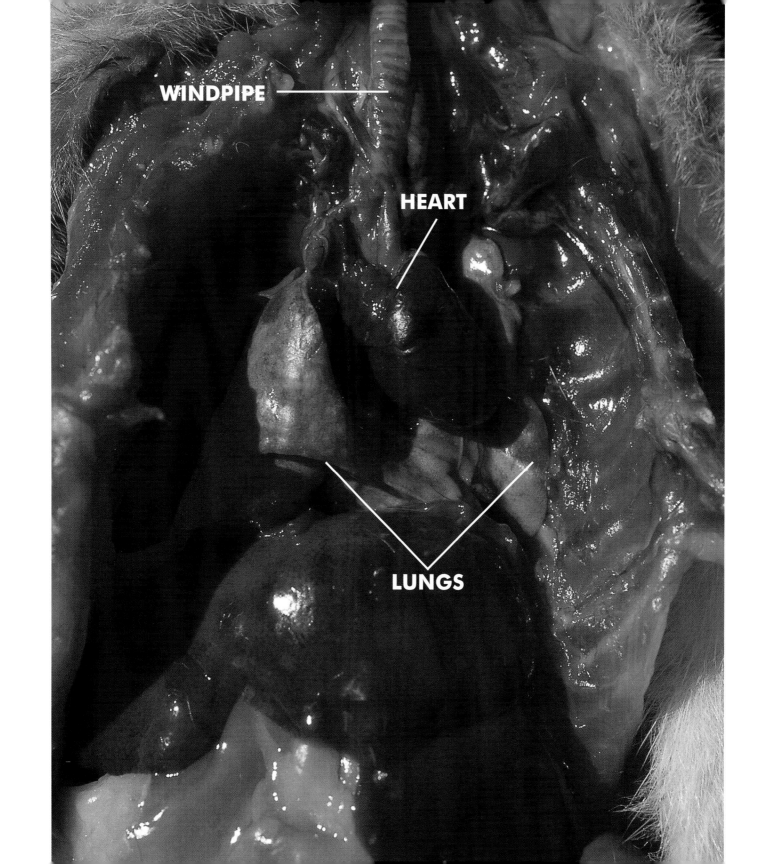

To make use of the food nutrients, a rat needs a steady supply of *oxygen,* one of the gases in the air. Oxygen combines with food nutrients to release the energy the rat needs to be active, stay warm, and grow. Like you, when a rat breathes in, air flows down the windpipe to the *lungs.* There oxygen is exchanged for waste gas, *carbon dioxide.* Then the rat breathes out this waste gas.

The rat's blood carries oxygen and nutrients through its body. The pump that pushes the blood is a special muscle, the *heart.* But a rat does not control its heartbeat the way it does its running or jumping. The heart has a built-in pacemaker that keeps it beating. The rat's *brain* controls how fast or slow the heart pumps—fast when active, slow while resting.

The jumping mouse lives where the nuts and berries it eats are hard to find during the winter. So as the days grow shorter and colder, the mouse carries home nuts stuffed in its cheeks. It also eats more than it needs to be active, so some of the nutrients are stored in its body as fat.

Finally, the mouse finds a cozy spot out of the wind. There it builds a nest of leaves and straw and curls up. Its heart rate and breathing slows. This special deep sleep, called *hibernation,* lets the jumping mouse live through the winter on its stored fat.

This jumping mouse has curled up for the winter.

What could these rats be doing?

Did you guess that the two rats were fighting? When they fight, rats usually stand upright and look like they're boxing. They also bite and seem to be screaming, but some of the sounds they make are too high-pitched for human ears to hear. Most often, males fight males and females fight females. Winning means getting first choice for a mate or food. The fight ends when one rat signals it gives up by lying down on its back.

Look at the newborn brown rats. Rats and mice often have a *litter*, or lots of babies at one time. How many babies do you see in this litter?

Rats will mate at any time of year as long as there is plenty of food. They are ready to begin having babies when they are only about three months old.

Whenever rats mate, a cell from a male, called a *sperm,* joins with the female's *egg* cell. Then the young, or *embryo,* begins to develop inside the mother in a special body part called a *womb.* Birth, the moment when the baby rat is born, happens after about twenty-one days. Before you were born, you developed about two hundred and seventy days—nine months.

Look at the soft straw nest this white-footed mouse made for her babies. Did you see the rat's paper nest on page 28? Rats and mice chew up what they can find to build comfortable places to sleep or to raise their babies.

Brown rats live together in a group called a *colony*. They dig an underground home with chambers to store food and to drop their body wastes. They also build nursery chambers where mothers raise their young. There are rarely any orphans in a rat colony. If a mother dies, nearby females adopt her babies.

Did you guess this mother rat is giving her day-old baby a bath?

Blind, deaf, and hairless, newborn baby brown rats are helpless. A sense of smell guides the babies to their mother's nipples and the waiting milk supply. The baby rats make soft squeaks as they suck. They'll nurse often for the first week. When they're full and sleepy, Mom licks each baby clean. If the nest material becomes soiled, Mom carries out the old and brings in fresh material.

These baby rats are just seven days old. Look how they've changed since they were born.

See the hint of a fur coat? At first, the naked babies had to depend on Mom's body heat to warm them. Soon their fur coat will keep them warm. By the end of the second week, the babies' ears will open so they can hear. By the end of the third week, their eyes will open so they can see.

Just six weeks old, this white-footed mouse is on its own. Mom wouldn't let it nurse any longer so the youngster will have to find its own food. This is the most dangerous time for the young mouse because it has not yet learned where to search. It also doesn't know which trails are safe. If it survives for a few weeks, it will be ready to find a mate and then begin to produce babies of its own.

Clearly, rats and mice are special . . . from the inside out!

GLOSSARY/INDEX

NOTE: Glossary words are italicized the first time they appear in the text.

BLOOD blud: The fluid that flows through a rat's body, carrying food nutrients and oxygen to all body parts and wastes away. **13, 23**

BONES bōnz: The hard but lightweight parts that form the body's supporting frame. **6, 15**

BRAIN brān: Body part that receives messages about what is happening inside and outside the body. It sends messages to put the body into action. **23**

CARBON DIOXIDE kär'-bən dī-ok-sid: A gas that is given off naturally in body activities, carried to the lungs by the blood, and breathed out. **23**

COLONY kol'ə-nē: A group of rats or mice living together and sharing the same area. **31**

DIGESTION dī-jes'chən: The process of chemicals breaking down food. **20**

EGG eg: Female reproductive cell. **29**

EMBRYO em'-brē-ō: Name given to the young developing in the womb. **29**

ENAMEL i-nam'əl: The tough outer layer on teeth. The back surface of a rat's front teeth is softer than the front. So it wears away faster as the rat gnaws, giving the tooth a sharp, chisel shape. **6**

GNAW nä: Scraping and biting process rats and mice use to chew through really tough materials. **6**

HEART härt: Body part that acts like a pump, constantly pushing blood throughout the rat's body. **23, 24**

HIBERNATION hībər-nā-chən: The sort of sleep state a rat or a mouse is in when its heart and breathing rate slows. This lets the animal survive harsh environmental conditions. Not all rats and mice hibernate. **24**

LARGE INTESTINE lärj in-tes'-tin: Here most of the water remaining in the wastes passes back into the bloodstream. **20**

LITTER lit'ər: A group of young produced at the same time by one mother. **28**

LUNG ləng: Body part where oxygen and carbon dioxide are exchanged. **23**

MUSCLES məs'-əlz: Working in pairs, muscles move the rat's bones by pulling on them. **15, 23**

NEST nest: A snug retreat where rats and mice sleep or raise their young. **9, 24, 30**

NUTRIENTS nü-trē-əntz: Chemical building blocks into which food is broken down for use by the rat's body. The five basic nutrients provided by food are proteins, fats, carbohydrates, minerals, and vitamins. **20, 23**

OXYGEN ok'-si-jən: A gas in the air that is breathed into the lungs, carried by the blood throughout the body, and combined with food nutrients to release energy. **23**

SALIVA sə-lī'-və: Liquid produced in the mouth that helps the digestion process. **20**

SKELETON skel'-ə-tən: The framework of bones that supports the body and gives it its shape. **15**

SMALL INTESTINE smäl in-tes'-tin: The tube-shaped body part where food is mixed with special digestive juices to break it down into nutrients. The nutrients then pass through the walls into the bloodstream. **20**

SPERM spᵿrm: The male reproductive cell. **29**

STOMACH stəm'-ək: Tubelike body part where bacteria break down much of the plant material before it is passed into the small intestine. **20**

URINE yur' in: Liquid body wastes. **18**

WOMB wüm: Female body part where the embryo develops before birth. **29**

LOOKING BACK

1. Look closely at the whiskers of the brown rat on the title page. Can you guess why these sensitive hairs stick out farther than any part of its body? (Check page 16 for a clue.)

2. Take another look at the brown rats dining on page 2. Brown rats are very social. They recognize the scent and sounds of other rats in their colony. They're quick to attack outsiders.

3. On page 8, use a ruler to measure the length of the mouse's tail and its body. Which is longer? By how much?

4. How old do you think the brown rat baby is on page 12—a few days, two weeks, or four weeks? Look at the babies on pages 32, 34, and 36 to help you decide.

5. Check out the mouse's big eyes on page 18. Mice and rats have eyes that let in as much light as possible—just right for seeing well in dim light.

6. It's Mom that is washing the babies on page 32. Father rats usually don't care for the babies.

PHOTO CREDITS

COVER:	Dwight Khun
TITLE PG:	Jane Burton/Bruce Coleman
p. 2	Jane Burton/Bruce Coleman
p. 4	Dwight Kuhn
p. 5	Rod Williams/Bruce Coleman
p. 6	John Visser/Bruce Coleman
p. 7	Dwight Kuhn
p. 8	Dwight Kuhn
p. 9	Sandra Markle
p. 10	Kim Tayler/Bruce Coleman
p. 12	Kim Taylor/Bruce Coleman
p. 13	Sandra Markle
p. 14	Sandra Markle (X ray)
p. 16	Robin Redfern/Oxford Scientific Films
p. 17	Dwight Kuhn
p. 18	Dwight Kuhn
p. 19	Dwight Kuhn
p. 21	Sandra Markle
p. 22	Sandra Markle
p. 25	John Serrao
p. 26	Jen and Des Bartlett/Bruce Coleman
p. 28	Jane Burton/Bruce Coleman
p. 30	Dwight Kuhn
p. 31	Jane Burton/Bruce Coleman
p. 32	Jane Burton/Bruce Coleman
p. 34	Jane Burton/Bruce Coleman
p. 36	Dwight Kuhn

ä as in c**a**rt   ā as in **a**pe   ə as in b**a**nan**a**   ē as in **e**ven   ī as in b**i**te

ō as in g**o**   ü as in r**u**le   ʉ as in f**u**r

For my dear friends Dave and Phyllis Brown

The author would like to thank the following for sharing their expertise and enthusiasm: Fred Alvey, Zoo Atlanta, and Dr. Wallace Dawson, South Carolina State University.

ATHENEUM BOOKS FOR YOUNG READERS
An imprint of Simon & Schuster Children's Publishing Division
1230 Avenue of the Americas
New York, New York 10020
Text copyright © 2001 by Sandra Markle
The text of this book is set in Melior.
Printed in Hong Kong
2 4 6 8 10 9 7 5 3 1
Library of Congress Cataloging-in-Publication Data
Markle, Sandra.
Outside and inside rats and mice / by Sandra Markle.—1st ed.
        p.   cm.
ISBN 0-689-82301-0
1. Rats—Juvenile literature. 2. Mice—Juvenile literature. 3. Rats—Anatomy—Juvenile literature.
4. Mice—Anatomy—Juvenile literature. [1. Rats. 2. Mice.] I. Title.
QL737.R666 M27 2001
599.35—dc21   00-029290

FIRST
EDITION